Wolf Hill

Electric Sandwiches

Roderick Hunt

Illustrated by Alex Brychta

Oxford University Press

OXFORD
UNIVERSITY PRESS
Great Clarendon Street, Oxford OX2 6DP

Oxford New York
Athens Auckland Bangkok Bogotá Buenos Aires Calcutta
Cape Town Chennai Dar es Salaam Delhi Florence Hong Kong Istanbul
Karachi Kuala Lumpur Madrid Melbourne Mexico City Mumbai
Nairobi Paris São Paulo Singapore Taipei Tokyo Toronto Warsaw

and associated companies in Berlin Ibadan

First Published 1999

ISBN 0 19 918741 X

Printed in Hong Kong

Chapter 1

The new boy was small and thin. His face was pale and his hair looked dirty. He wore scruffy jeans and an old sweater.

He came into Miss Teal's class with Mr Saffrey. Nobody liked the look of him.

'This is Zak,' said Mr Saffrey. 'Where do you want him to sit?'

'I don't know,' said Miss Teal. 'We're working in groups. Zak can sit at my table for now.'

Everyone looked at Zak. Nobody smiled at him.

'He's a dip-stick,' said Michael Ward.

'Shut up, Wardy,' said Kat. 'Don't be so horrid.'

Zak sat at Miss Teal's table. He didn't move. He didn't look at anyone. He just sniffed a lot. In the end, Miss Teal gave him a tissue.

Then Zak got a sheet of paper with squares on. He began to colour each square with a crayon.

'I said he was a dip-stick,' said Michael Ward.

‘Well, I feel sorry for him,’ said Kat.
‘But why?’ asked Andy.
‘I don’t know,’ said Kat. ‘I just do.’

Chapter 2

At break, Zak had vanished.

Michael Ward looked round the playground. 'Where's that new kid?' he called. 'Who's seen Zak?'

Kat went up to Michael Ward. 'Just leave Zak alone,' she said.

'What do you mean?' said Michael Ward. 'I haven't touched him.' He looked at his friends. 'Have I done anything to the new kid?' he asked.

'Well don't,' said Kat.

Gizmo spoke to Kat. 'I know where Zak is,' he said. 'He's hiding.'

'Where?' said Kat.

Gizmo pointed to an area near the kitchen. It was out of bounds. By the wall were two big plastic bins.

'Zak's in there,' said Gizmo. 'He's hiding between those two bins.'

'Why is he hiding?' asked Loz.

'I think he scared,' said Kat. 'He's scared of being teased.'

'Do you think we should leave him?' said Loz.

Najma looked at her watch. 'We've got swimming next,' she said.

'We'd better tell Miss Teal, then,' said Loz.

Chapter 3

Andy searched through his bag. He looked under his clothes. His towel was missing.

Chris and Gizmo were still drying themselves. Gizmo looked cold. He had his towel round him like a cloak.

‘That’s odd,’ said Andy. ‘I can’t find my towel.’

Gizmo and Chris looked along the bench. Gizmo asked, 'Has anyone seen Andy's towel?'

Miss Teal banged on the door. 'Hurry up,' she called.

Andy felt cold. He began to shiver.

'I bet you forgot it,' said Chris. He threw his own towel at Andy. 'Borrow mine,' he said.

Andy remembered something else. He had worn his swimming trunks to school. He remembered putting a clean pair of pants in his towel.

Andy didn't know what to do. He didn't want to tell Miss Teal. She might tell him off. He was not supposed to wear his swimming trunks to school. He knew that.

The underpants had wombats on them. They were brand new. Miss Teal might ask what they looked like. She might start a search.

It was a mystery. His towel and his wombat underpants had vanished.

Chapter 4

After swimming, everyone is always hungry. Andy, Chris and Gizmo have sandwiches. So do Kat, Loz and Najma. They sit together.

Gizmo makes his own sandwiches. One day he put hundreds and thousands on some bread. That's how he invented the electric sandwich.

The hundreds and thousands melted. The colours soaked into the bread. Gizmo made sandwiches with the bread.

'I call them electric sandwiches,' he said. 'They give you a shock when you see them.'

Everyone laughed. They wanted to swap sandwiches with Gizmo.

After that, Gizmo often made electric sandwiches.

Today something odd happened. Gizmo opened his lunch box. His electric sandwiches were missing.

'Strange!' said Gizmo. 'My sandwiches aren't here. I'm sure I put them in.'

'You must have left them at home,' said Najma. 'Have one of mine.'

Chris looked in his lunch box. 'That's funny,' he said. 'My chocolate bar has gone. Someone's taken it.'

'Don't be silly,' said Kat. 'Who would steal sandwiches and a chocolate bar?'

Chapter 5

Miss Teal was putting up a display. She clapped her hands. 'There's too much noise,' she said.

Everyone had work to do. They had to finish their topics.

‘If you’ve finished,’ said Miss Teal, ‘get your reading books out.’

She looked at Zak. He didn’t have a book.

‘Loz,’ said Miss Teal, ‘show Zak where the reading books are. Then he can sit next to you.’

‘Oh no!’ whispered Loz. ‘I don’t like Zak. He smells.’

Zak kept sniffing. Loz sighed. She gave him a tissue. ‘Blow your nose,’ she said.

The bell went. Miss Teal made everyone leave quietly. ‘Have a nice weekend,’ she said.

Loz looked for her tissues. ‘That’s funny,’ she said. ‘I can’t find my tissues. I know I had some. I gave one to Zak.’

Something clicked in Andy’s mind.

He thought of all the missing things. ‘I may be wrong,’ he said. ‘But I think someone’s stealing things.’

Najma looked in her bag. ‘Oh no!’ she said. ‘My watch has gone.’

Chapter 6

Najma looked in her bag again. 'I'm sure I put my watch in here,' she said. 'Now it's gone.'

She gave the bag to Loz. 'You have a look,' she said.

Loz looked in the bag. 'It isn't here,' she said.

'All kinds of things have gone missing,' said Andy. 'I lost my towel this morning.'

'Gizmo's electric sandwiches have gone,' said Chris. 'And so has my chocolate bar.'

'My tissues went missing,' said Loz.

'But these are funny things to steal,' said Andy. 'Who would want to take them?'

'Could it be Zak?' asked Chris. 'He was at the pool, but he didn't swim. He could have taken Andy's towel when we were swimming. He could have taken Gizmo's sandwiches, too.'

Najma frowned. 'Do you think he took my watch?' she said.

'There's one way to be sure,' said Loz. 'Find Zak and ask him.'

‘It’s no good,’ said Andy. ‘He will have gone home by now.’

‘It’s worth a try,’ said Najma. ‘Loz and Andy! Run to the front gate! Chris and I will try the playground. It may still not be too late!’

Chapter 7

Zak hadn't gone home. He was still in the playground. Michael Ward had his bag.

Zak's face looked white. 'Give me my bag,' he shouted.

Michael Ward held the bag up high. 'Come and get it,' he called. Zak ran at him. But Michael Ward threw the bag to a friend.

The bag sailed through the air. It went from friend to friend. 'Come on, Zak,' someone yelled. 'Zak attack! Zak attack! Zak attack!'

Michael Ward caught the bag. He threw it up in the air. A girl ran to catch it.

Suddenly Kat ran up. She jumped high and caught the bag. Then she gave it to Zak. 'Here you are,' she said.

'Spoilsport,' shouted Michael Ward.

Zak grabbed his bag. Then he raced across the playground. Something fell out of his bag.

Then Chris and Najma came out of the school. 'Zak!' called Chris. 'Come back! We want to talk to you.'

Zak didn't stop. He ran out of the gate.

Chris looked serious. He picked something up. 'Look what dropped out of Zak's bag,' he said. 'Gizmo's electric sandwiches!'

Chapter 8

'This proves he's been taking things,' said Chris.

'He may have my watch,' said Najma.

'That's terrible,' said Kat. 'Quick! Let's run after him. Maybe we can catch him up.'

Kat, Chris and Najma ran into Wolf Street. At first they couldn't see Zak. Then they saw him running along Canal Street. They began to chase him.

Chris wasn't good at running. He couldn't keep up. 'Chris! Go back and get Miss Teal,' yelled Kat.

'OK,' puffed Chris.

Zak ran down the track at the end of Canal Street. The track led to the allotments.

‘He’s heading for the canal path,’ panted Najma.

Kat and Najma raced down the track. Then they stopped. There was no sign of Zak. He had vanished. A dog began to bark madly.

‘He’s hiding somewhere,’ said Najma. ‘He must be behind a shed.’

'There are lots of sheds here,' said Kat. 'He could be anywhere.'

Suddenly, a dog jumped over a fence. It raced towards them, growling and snapping. Kat screamed.

'Run!' shouted Najma.

Chapter 9

Najma sprinted towards a shed. Kat followed. The dog ran at them.

Some old boxes were leaning against the shed. Kat and Najma climbed up the boxes and scrambled on to the roof.

Kat was shaking with fright.

The dog leaped against the boxes. The top one fell down, and the dog backed away. Then it ran at the shed again.

Zak came from nowhere. He put his fingers in his mouth and whistled. The whistle had a high, thin sound. The dog stopped barking. It looked at Zak and crouched down very low.

There was a broken rope round the dog's neck. Zak tied the rope to a post. He looked at Kat and Najma.

'You can get down now,' he said.

Kat and Najma climbed down. Kat was still shaking.

'Thanks, Zak,' said Najma. 'Is that your dog?'

'I've never seen him before,' said Zak.

'But how did you make him stop?' asked Najma.

'I'm good with dogs, that's all,' said Zak.

Just then, Chris and Miss Teal arrived.

Chapter 10

Miss Teal asked Zak to open his bag. She looked at the things inside it. There was a chocolate bar, some tissues, and a towel with Andy's wombat underpants.

'Why did you take such odd things?' she asked.

Zak sniffed. 'My mum's ill in bed,' he said. 'She can't look after us. We haven't got any money. We haven't got anything.'

'Where do you live?' asked Najma.

'We live in Hacket Green,' said Zak. 'Just Mum and me, and my little sister.'

'Let's go back to school,' said Miss Teal. 'If your mum is ill, we can get help.'

‘No!’ shouted Zak. ‘They’ll put us in a home. We don’t want to go into care.’

Suddenly Zak spun round and ran. He sprinted across the allotments. The dog barked and jerked on the rope.

Zak raced towards the canal.

‘Shall we go after him?’ said Chris.

‘No. Let him go,’ said Miss Teal.

Chapter 11

'What about my watch?' asked Najma. 'It isn't in Zak's bag.'

'That's why we chased Zak in the first place,' said Chris.

'He didn't take it,' said Miss Teal. 'I found it in the classroom. Najma left it in her tray.'

'Oh dear,' said Najma. 'I thought Zak had it. Now I feel terrible.'

Just then, a man shouted, 'Hey! What are you doing with my dog?' He ran up and grabbed the dog's rope.'

'He chased us,' said Kat. 'We were scared.'

The man looked at the broken rope. 'I'm sorry,' he said. 'He's a bit lively. He must have broken free.'

Miss Teal put the things back in Zak's bag. A piece of paper fell to the ground.

Kat picked it up and looked at it. It was the piece of paper with squares on it. Zak had spent all day colouring it in.

'I feel even more sorry for Zak now,' said Kat.

Zak had made a pattern. In the middle was one word. It said *'Mum'*.

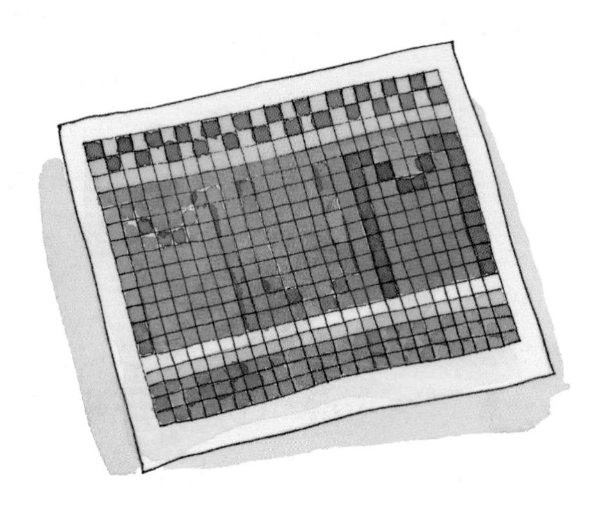

Chapter 12

Later, Miss Teal called at Najma's house. She had Najma's watch. Mrs Patel went to the door.

'Did Najma tell you that a dog chased her?' said Miss Teal. 'I came to see if she was all right.'

'She's fine,' said Mrs Patel. 'She told me about a boy called Zak.'

'I've been to his home,' said Miss Teal. 'I went to take his bag back. His mother is ill. She's finding it hard to cope. She needs to see a doctor.'

'Well, I'm a nurse,' said Mrs Patel. 'Do you want me to call and see her?'

Najma was listening. 'They need food and stuff,' she said. 'That's why Zak took Gizmo's sandwiches.'

'I'll take some things round,' said Mrs Patel. 'Zak saved Najma and Kat from that dog. I'd like to help him.'

'That would be kind,' said Miss Teal.

Najma and Mrs Patel called on Kat's mum. 'We're going to Zak's flat,' said Mrs Patel. 'We've got some food and a few clothes for them.'

'I'll come with you,' said Mrs Wilson. 'I'll see if I can help.'

'May Kat come, too?' asked Najma.

'Well, I suppose so,' said Mrs Wilson.

Chapter 13

Hacket Green was the other side of the Wolf Hill Road. There was writing on the walls of the flats.

Mrs Patel rang the door bell. She rang and rang. There was no answer.

A woman in the next flat opened her door.

'They've gone,' she said. 'They're on the run again. You won't see them again.'

'But why have they gone?' asked Kat.

'It's sad,' said Mrs Wilson. 'I guess Zak's mum was afraid.'

'Afraid of what?' asked Najma.

'Of her children being taken away,' said Mrs Patel. 'She thought they might be put in a home.'

'It doesn't seem fair,' said Najma.

Chapter 14

On Monday, Najma and Kat told the others about Zak.

'I know he stole things,' said Najma, 'but he did it to help his family.'

‘Does that make it all right?’ said Gizmo. ‘Stealing is stealing.’

‘I just don’t know,’ said Andy.

‘He was a strange kid,’ said Loz.

‘He loved his mum,’ said Kat. ‘And the way he handled that dog was amazing.’

‘I don’t think we’ll see him again,’ said Najma.

Everyone thought of Zak and his sister. What would happen to them? Would they go to a new school?

Gizmo bit into one of his electric sandwiches.

'Some kids have hard lives,' he said.